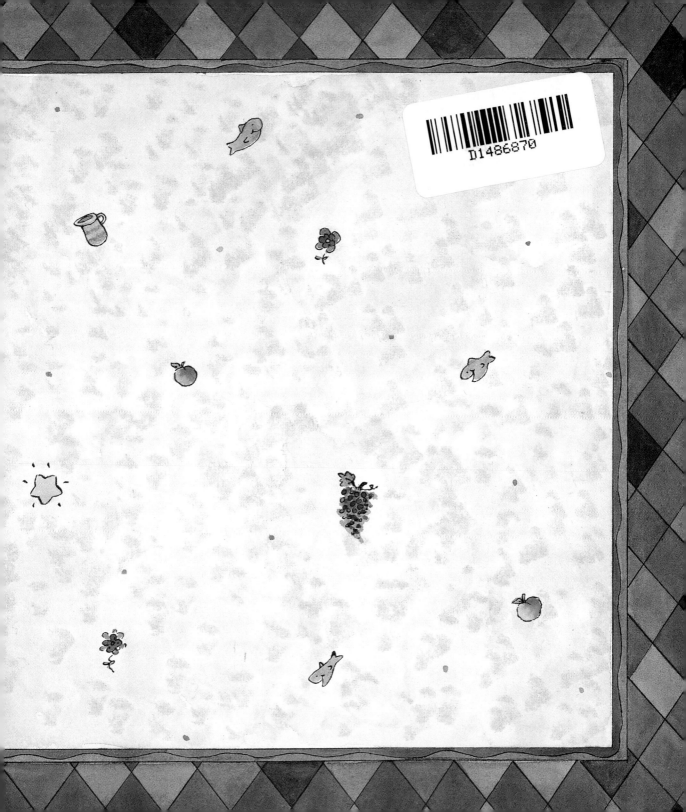

The Standard Publishing Company, Cincinnati, Ohio
A division of Standex International Corporation
© 1994 by The Standard Publishing Company
All rights reserved.
Printed in the United States of America
01 00 99 98 97 96 95 94   5 4 3 2 1

Library of Congress Catalog Card Number 93-5386
Cataloging-in-Publication data available
Designed by Coleen Davis
Typography by Andy Rector

Standard Publishing
Cincinnati, Ohio

Friends from GALILEE

BY DANA STEWART

A BIBLE-TIMES VISIT WITH MICAH AND HANNAH

ILLUSTRATED BY KATHY COURI

Hi! My name is Micah.
I am six.
This is my sister Hannah.
Hannah is four.
We came to the market
this morning to buy
these grapes.
We need
to hurry home now.
I think I can hear
our mother calling us.
Hey, I have an idea —
why don't you
come home with us!

We live in the village
of Bethsaida,
near the Sea of Galilee.
Here is our house.
It is small,
but we have
an outdoor courtyard
where we often
work and play.
And eat!
See — Mother has food
ready for us —
bread, honey, and milk
from our goat.
Would you like some?

This is our mother,
Rachel,
and our baby sister, Joanna.

Our father's name is Simon.
He is a fisherman.
He has been out fishing

on the Sea of Galilee
since before the sun was up.
He will come home

after he cleans his nets
and takes the fish
to the market.

Please come
inside. I will
show you our
house.

My father built our house from clay.
He made our benches and table too.
Would you like to sit down?

Look inside this bushel —
that's where we keep our food!

In the morning we roll up our sleeping mats
and put them in this space in the wall.
At night, when it gets dark, we light this lamp.

Every day we all
have work to do.
Hannah watches baby Joanna
while Mother
bakes bread.
Mother also takes this jar
to the well to get water.
She carries it
on her head,
like this!

Father fishes, cleans his nets,
and sells his fish.
I feed the animals.
You can help me.
Here is our goat,
our sheep,
and our chickens.
They are hungry today!

When my chores are done,
it is time for me
to go to school.
Hannah is too young
for school.
She will stay home
and help Mother
cook and sew.
I like school.
I see my friends there.
We have to walk,
but it isn't far.
Let's run —
we don't want to be late!

Sit here on the floor
beside me.
This is our teacher.
His name is Benjamin,
but we call him
rabbi.
Rabbi means
"teacher."
Rabbi is
teaching us
to read the Scriptures.
We are learning
about numbers too.
I can count
to fifty now —
can you?

When school is over, I am hungry. Are you?

Look what Mother has ready for us —
fresh bread, cheese, figs,

and the grapes Hannah and I bought at the market.

And here is mutton and vegetable stew,
cooking for dinner tonight.
Mmmm, it smells good!

In the afternoon, the day grows so hot!
Would you like to cool off in the sea?
Last year Father taught me how to swim.
Watch me kick!
Come on in — the water feels fine!

That was fun! Now let's play
with my ball. Good catch!

Let's go up on the roof and watch
for Father coming home.
I'll race you up the stairs!

Our roof is flat.
Guests can sleep here.
This little wall keeps
them from falling off.
I like to come up
on the roof
and look out over
the whole village.
There is Father now.
And he has
relatives with him!

This is Father and our Aunt Naomi . . .

and Uncle Solomon and our cousin Abraham.

Father has asked them to come in and visit.

Hannah will bring
them water
to wash the dust
off their feet.
You and I
will feed and water
their donkey.
Mother will have
supper ready
soon.

Father has wonderful news —
Jesus is on his way to our village!

Do you know Jesus?
He tells wonderful stories.
Father says Jesus was sent to us by God.

Look — he is coming now!

Hurry! I don't want to miss *anything* he says.

Wow! What a great day! Hannah and I are
so glad to have you for a new friend.
And we *all* get to see Jesus!

Thanks for visiting with us today.
Please come back soon!